© 1995 Geddes & Grosset Ltd
Published by Geddes & Grosset Ltd,
New Lanark, Scotland.

ISBN 1 85534 584 6

Printed and bound in Great Britian.

The Three Wishes

Retold by Judy Hamilton
Illustrated by Lindsay Duff

Tarantula Books

Once upon a time in a small cottage at the edge of the forest, there lived a woodcutter and his wife. They did not have a lot of money and they both had to work very hard to earn their living. Sometimes, when they sat together by the fire at night, they would pretend that they had three wishes:

"If I had three wishes," the woodcutter would begin, "I would wish for....."

Then his wife would join in and choose her three wishes. With each game, the wishes were different, but this was part of the fun. And so it was that they whiled away many long winter evenings, making one make-believe wish after another.

One day, as the woodcutter worked away deep in the forest, chopping wood, something strange happened. He was just lifting his axe, ready to cut down an old oak tree, when a tiny little man appeared. It was one of the magic sprites that lived in the forest.

"Please, woodcutter, spare this tree!" he cried. "This tree has been my home for one hundred years. If you chop it down, I shall have nowhere to live!"

The woodcutter felt sorry for the sprite, but he also wanted to chop down the tree. He did not know what to do. The sprite spoke again:

"If you will spare this tree, then I will give you three wishes," he said.

When he heard this, the old woodcutter was delighted. Three wishes! Three REAL wishes!

"Very well," he told the sprite, "I will spare the tree."

"Thank you, kind woodcutter," said the sprite. "I do not know where I would go if I did not have my dear old tree to live in, and I am very grateful to you. You may have your three wishes, but I advise you to use them carefully. Whenever you say the words 'I wish', whatever you say after that will come true. So think before you speak!"

"Oh, indeed I will!" said the woodcutter. "Thank you so much! I must get home now, and tell my wife all about this!"

The woodcutter picked up his axe and set off for home at once and the sprite vanished into the depths of the old oak tree.

When the woodcutter reached his cottage, he dropped his axe at the front door and rushed inside to tell his wife the exciting news. The old woman was in the middle of preparing supper.

"This is wonderful news indeed," she said when her husband had told her about the three wishes, "and it could bring us great good fortune. But we must think carefully before we make our wishes. Let us have our supper first. We will think much more clearly when our stomachs are full."

"What a sensible woman you are," the woodcutter said. "What's for supper?"

The woodcutter's wife took the lid from the pot that was bubbling on the fire and showed him what was cooking. It was a tasty barley broth. But the woodcutter was not impressed.

"What? No meat?" he said.

"We have not made our fortune yet," his wife said. "We cannot afford meat every day."

"What a pity," said the woodcutter, "for I am particularly hungry this evening."

He sighed heavily and looked back into the soup pot. Then, dreamily, he looked at the smoke curling up the chimney from the cooking fire.

"A sausage would have been nice with our soup," he said.

"A big, fat juicy sausage would be nice," he repeated. "Oh, how I wish that a great big fat juicy sausage could come flying down the chimney and into the soup pot."

The woodcutter realised at once what he had done and clapped his hands over his mouth. But it was too late. There was a tremendous "WHOOSH!" as the startled old man and his wife saw the most enormous sausage come shooting down the chimney and land in the pot of barley broth, "SPLASH!"

The woodcutter's wife was furious.

"What have you done, you stupid man?" she screamed. "Just look at all this mess!"

The woodcutter's wife had never been so angry.

"You have wasted one of our precious wishes!" she cried in despair. "Now we only have two wishes left and we will have to think even more carefully if we are to make the best of them. Oh, how could you have been so stupid?"

The woodcutter listened to his wife's angry shouts with a face as red as a beetroot.

Desperately, he tried to think of a way to calm her down.

"I have been very foolish, I know," he said, "so I think you should decide yourself what the next wish should be. You will be able to put it to the best use. Now please, let us sit down and have our supper in peace before we do another thing."

The woodcutter's wife sat down at the table. It was nice to think that the second wish was all hers, but her anger at the waste of the first wish was still smouldering away. Silently she watched her husband lift the soup pot from the fire and set it on the table in front of her. Not a word did she say as he ladled out the steaming liquid into two bowls and handed her one of them. But then the woodcutter turned to her timidly and asked,

"Would you like a piece of the sausage, my dear? It looks very tasty, after all!" and she lost her temper again.

She pushed her chair away from the table with a clatter.

"Sausage?" she screeched, "SAUSAGE? You and that stupid fat old sausage have cost us one of our precious wishes! Of course I don't want a piece of sausage. You can have the sausage all to yourself. It was you that wished for it and you are welcome to it!"

Then the woodcutter's wife fished the sausage out of the soup pot and waved it in the air in front of her miserable husband.

"In fact," she shouted angrily, " I wish this stupid sausage would go and stick itself on the end of your nose!"

"NO!" shouted the woodcutter.

"Oh help!" moaned his wife.

Of course, the woodcutter's wife could not take her words back. Once she had said "I wish," there was no way that she could stop it from happening. She tried to hold on tightly to the sausage, but it wriggled out of her grasp. It swooped across the room gracefully and attached itself to the tip of the woodcutter's nose.

The woodcutter looked down his nose in dismay. He tried to pull the sausage off but it was stuck firm. He tried to twist it off but he only hurt his nose. He thought about cutting it off but he was too afraid that it might hurt even more. In the end he gave up and slumped down in his chair feeling wretched.

His wife began to cry.

"Oh dear, oh dear," she sobbed. "Two wishes gone and all that we have to show for it is a big fat sausage on the end of your nose. How foolish we have been. What shall we wish for with our third wish, my dear? How can we get it right this time?"

The woodcutter looked at his wife.

"Well my dear," he said, "I am sure that you do not want to spend the rest of your life with a man who has a sausage stuck to the end of his nose. And I certainly do not want to remain looking like this for ever. So I can only think of one use for the last wish. It will not bring us good fortune, but at least it will leave us no worse off than we were before."

The woodcutter's wife smiled at him through her tears and nodded.

"You are right my dear," she said, "it is the only way to use the last wish. Shall we do it together?"

So the woodcutter and his wife closed their eyes and wished, and the sausage disappeared. With a sigh of relief the old couple sat down and ate their soup in contented silence.

In years to come, the woodcutter and his wife were able to remember that day and laugh. They had wasted three wishes, but they had learned from their mistakes that they did not need wishes to make them happy. They were already happy enough in the life that they had together.